I0611700

Dead or Alive A Fall From Grace
Second edition
A short Story
Author - Kilene 'Ki' Williams

Book 3 in the
I Am My Sister's Keeper series

Publisher: Bleeding Ink Creatives, LLC

ISBN: 978-1-7366315-3-9

Acknowledgements
To my village, you know without hesitation exactly who you are. I thank you from the depths of my soul. I love you, and there is absolutely nothing you can do about it!

To my readers, thank you for indulging in my writing wilds. Your support is appreciated. May you have the courage to release your creativity and make your dreams reality.

Chapter 1

Cher

I inherited twenty-five million dollars from my paternal grandfather. Although I've never met him, he always knew who and where I was. Unable to raise me or be considered for custody, he wrote me a letter with his last will and testament and explained why he had to keep his distance. He asked for my forgiveness and left me his entire estate.

I had a lot to wrap my brain around without the opportunity to speak to my grandfather and hear the millions of questions swirling in my psyche answered firsthand. He left me an estate which included my beautiful home on Beachfront avenue and a stunning yacht. I named the yacht *The Bourbon Princess*. Well, the yacht isn't stunning anymore, it was blown to smithereens. I still have nightmares about the explosion. It's hard to believe that's how we lost Pierre. He would do anything to protect Victoria and Sade, literally anything.

My grandfather also left in trust an additional fifteen million dollars to be divided amongst my immediate heirs if I have children.

Growing up in the foster care system left me with a lasting mood of distrust. I was simply a paycheck to every home I landed in no matter the circumstances. Victoria, Sade and Rae are my family, I have no one else I can truly count on. I thought I had Matthew, but that was me being naïve enough to think someone would actually want me, all of me, and stay.

What do you do when the man you shared all your hopes and dreams with takes your trust and loyalty for granted?

I put my guard down and gave Matthew all of me, only to be betrayed in the worst way, in my own home. Who does that? My sisterhood with my girls is everything to me. Where would I be right now if it weren't for Vic. My entire world has been turned upside down. Sade is beside herself with anger because she feels like she's the only reason Grace came into our lives in the first place. I know however, that everything happens for a reason, even if it's intended to break your heart into a million pieces. How could Matthew cheat on me with someone we all know. And in our home, that I will never comprehend. I relive that evening in my mind repeatedly a few times a day.

I found a way to share my heart with Sebastian and Matthew, two men that chose to take me for granted. Sebastian was a beast and after his death I made my peace with what our relationship was or wasn't.

I matured and made a name for myself in the restaurant industry. Food is life, for me. Cooking gave me the creative space I needed to thrive. I chose Matthew because I thought he was safe. A haven from the bullshit I went through with Sebastian. And he was, for a while at least. He changed and I didn't even realize it because I was so trusting and loyal. I thought it was okay to pour into my career abundantly. It was our future I was working towards. He motivated and encouraged me through both restaurant openings and all my endeavors. I too was that backbone for him.

I don't understand how Grace became an option. I find myself confused and blaming myself. But what am I at fault for? I never neglected him or our home. From my parents, grandfather, foster parents and the fucked-up ass men I've chosen to bring into my life, I'm over people. Of course the men didn't reveal that they were fucked up when they came to me in their shiny newly wrapped packaging, but underneath the surface, was a whole other story.

Sitting at the kitchen counter drinking my morning coffee with a splash of bourbon, my thoughts fade as I hear my angel shuffling her way down the stairs.

"Good morning, Vic. How'd you sleep?"

"Better than you Cher. I heard you pacing all night."

"Touché Vic."

"Get your mind together Cher. Rae called to inform me that Stephen's friend Jayden has invited us to fly back home on his private jet with him for the fortieth birthday party. We leave tomorrow."

"Tomorrow, Vic? Why am I just hearing about this? I forgot Stephen's birthday was approaching." Vic looked at me with her no excuses glare in her eyes and continued.

"Yes ma'am, a little Florida sun will do the body good." Vic rolled her eyes at me and smiled.

"Yeah, if you say so Vic. Besides, I do have some unfinished family business I need to take care of. I've put it off long enough and now that Matthew's gone, I have time to focus on it." I blew Vic a kiss and went up to enjoy a hot shower.

I've never told the girls what I know about my grandfather, mainly to protect them. Thank God, my grandfather is the one subject that was off limits with Matthew. I never told him the truth. Although my grandfather wasn't there for me in life, in death I understand his choices. I am his last heir and despite his absence in my life he has provided for me in ways I never imagined. Then there's the truth about my parents. I spent my life thinking they had abandoned me willingly, only to learn from my grandfather's letter that they were executed for refusing to give up my grandfather's location. My grandfather was a Navy SEAL. Wanting to be in control of the missions he was assigned, he became a private contract assassin. Fluent in several languages, he was never in one place for long. His web was cast internationally. Somehow someone got close enough to him to figure out that he had a daughter. My mother was his only child. Her mother died in labor, leaving my grandfather to raise my mother alone. He raised her like a soldier, so she knew how to handle herself.

Reading the words my grandfather wrote finally made me feel like I belonged, I had family that I could identify. I couldn't share it, but I knew. I knew and that's what matters. Fuck Matthew. I don't want anything from him, but for him to move the fuck on.

All packed and ready to go, I brought my luggage down and placed it at the front door. I went into the kitchen and made me a cup of coffee and went outside to sit by the pool before we left. Peace washes over me. Stephen's party was right on time. It's time for me to go back. Matthew will not keep me from home. Vic came out singing good morning with her coffee in hand.

"Good morning, Queen Victoria. Are we ready to head to the airport?" I got up to pour a little more coffee for the road.

"Yes, it's about that time." Vic looked at me softly and asked, "Are you sure you're ready to return Cher?"

"Vic, I'm good. Let's get out of here Vegas will survive without us for a bit."

I have a lot to sort out. But it's all worth it. I am going to pour my energy into work and becoming one with my new identity. While my real name is Cher, my grandfather gifted me the truth about my birth sir name. He loved me and I will make him proud. I don't care what he did for a living. He loved me enough to keep me away from him, no matter what I went through in foster care, I know it was better than being killed. I am changing my name. I want my last name to match my grandfather's. His letters said my father was an alcoholic and is the weak link that got he and my mother killed. All that is a part of a past I had nothing to do with. Most won't understand what my grandfather did for a living, but he never stopped loving me, and for that I am grateful. I've been raped by foster fathers and treated as if I'm disposable to the men I've chosen. I'm done. I'm focused on me and only me.

Our flight was smooth. Jayden had lunch catered for the flight and plenty of vino to keep me calm. Stephen and Rae just text to let us know they are here to pick us up. I told them I could have called a car for us, but Stephen refused. Vic was the first to exit the plane. I wanted to finish my last glass of bourbon before plastering a smile on my face and greeting Rae and Stephen. I am determined to enjoy my visit home and let loose at Stephen's fortieth.

Jayden came and sat beside me while I sipped the rest of my bourbon. At first, I didn't realize he was there. I was so deep in my feelings. He cleared his throat, startling me out of my trance.

"Are you okay Cher," he asked.

"I will be Jayden. I'm just enjoying my last bit of bourbon and thinking. I'll hurry, I'm sure you have better things to do than to wait for me to finish."

"No, Cher. Don't rush and please call me Jay."

"Okay Jay, will you still be in town after Stephen's party or are you flying out shortly after?"

"I'll be leaving the next day for San Diego. Why do you ask? Would you be interested in joining me? You look like you could use a little time off the grid. I don't mean to pry, but I can tell something is weighing heavy on your mind."

I finished my bourbon and took a deep breath. So much is weighing on my mind. How am I supposed to respond to this.

"I'd love to go with you, I've never been to San Diego, and I hear it's beautiful. I could use the time away."

And just like that, before I had time to think the decision was made. I don't know who I was fooling anyway thinking I was ready to return to Miami. Not that I want Matthew to control my emotions, but shit, reality is I am not ready to spend more time than I have to in Miami right now. The wounds are still too fresh, and I'm done denying the truth to myself about how devastated I was after catching Matthew with Grace. I mean really. I've done so much for that bastard to help him with his career. I gave everything I had to him, and now it's time for me to be everything to my damn self.

"You'll be doing me a favor Cher. I won't have to fly back cross country alone and it will give me time to get to know you better. We met briefly at

Sade and Javier's engagement party, but never had the opportunity to reconnect. I'll be there for a week, and I am more than happy to fly you back to Vegas when I leave," Jay looked at me with reassuring eyes.

Funny he had me at would you be interested.

"I'm in, it sounds perfect Jayden, I mean Jay." A genuine smile hasn't graced my face in a while. According to the stories we've heard from Stephen, Jay works hard and plays harder. A good time is what I need right now.

"Girl what the hell are you doing?" Rae peeped her head on the plane.

"I'm coming sis just had to finish my bourbon, you know I'm a sipper. Oh, my goodness Rae you're glowing. You look beautiful."

"Well, my Cher, your beautifully glowing friend needs to eat so let's go. I have more bourbon at the house," Rae said winking and smiling at Jay."

Blushing, I put my number in Jay's phone and got up. Rae smirked at me and told me to hurry up.

"What's up? Was my boy trying to shoot his shot," Stephen asked with a tone that made it clear he already knew the answer to the question.

"Oh wow, did I miss something?" My voice cracked as I spoke.

Jay interrupted, "No Cher, you didn't miss anything. Let's go."

We all piled into Stephen's truck and headed to the house. I think Jay was a little embarrassed by Stephen's outburst, but I'm glad he's riding with us. I know Rae said we were all staying with her and Stephen while in town, but now I realize that includes Jay too. Even Sade and Javier are staying with us while we are here. Sade assured us that momma Sophia would bring the twins over to see us while we are in town. I talked a good game in my head yesterday, but I'm probably not even going to drive by my house on this trip. Dreading the down time that will come later, I hope no one asks me how I'm feeling about Matthew or even utters Grace's name in my presence.

"Rae! Sis, you look like you're about to pop. I've missed you so much."

"Cher, trust me we have so much to catch up on, I have missed you too sis, but I know you needed the time away to regroup. Just know, whatever you need, I got you."

"Thanks Rae."

"You're always welcome Cher. I love you sis."

"Sade is at the house waiting for us. She can't wait to see you and Vic." Rae motioned for us to hurry. "Come on you know how Sade gets if she thinks we are later than necessary. She's a worrier."

"I hope she's ready for her little sis Rae. I miss my sweet Sade so much. I wonder if she knows that Victor was also invited to Stephen's party. I want her to get used to me being happy with someone other than Pierre. There are no labels, but I genuinely enjoy every minute I spend with Victor. His energy and drive push me to higher heights daily," Vic poured her feelings out.

"The way your face just lit up I think she'll see that you are happy. Don't worry Vic, Rae reassured."

When we arrived at the house Sade was waiting for us in the driveway. Vic and I jumped out of the car before Rae could put the car in park.

"What took so long for you to get here?" Sade asked looking at both of us.

"We had to wait for Cher and Jay to finish flirting," Rae blurted out.

I flicked Rae on the neck before she had a chance to jump back.

"You better be glad I'm pregnant, or I'd drag you into the gym and make you hold the bag," Rae said rolling her eyes at me and continued. "Now bring your asses so I can show you to your rooms and we can chill and catch up. Sade ordered food from Oceanside Seafood Bar & Grill, *the bar she was intending to run with Grace*, and Stephen has your whiskey ready for you."

Rae looked radiant. Pregnancy looks good on her. I've missed her and Sade so much but I'm still not ready to be in Miami. I'm grateful to Jay for inviting me to San Diego. I just have to figure out when I'm going to break it to the girls. They are going to be disappointed that I won't be in town too long. Since it's Jay maybe Stephen will help soften the blow. At least they know I'll be traveling with someone Stephen knows and trusts.

We dropped our bags off in our rooms and filed back downstairs to eat. I'm starving and I plan on drinking the night away so food is a must. I am so proud of Sade for getting Oceanside up and running on her own. She didn't need Grace's trifling ass anyway. I appreciate Sade kicking Grace to the curb after I caught Matthew cheating on me with her. I'll lend my expertise to Sade when needed.

Chapter 2

Jayden

In a perfect world the silence filtering through the air would be all that's needed to sleep peacefully. Not me though. I've tossed and turned for the last two hours. The sun will be up before I know it. All I can think about is Cher. She's such a savvy and shrewd businesswoman. From what Stephen told me she's been through hell and back and manages to pour all her energy into work and the people she loves, her sisters in life. I can respect an independent woman. I just hope she's not completely closed off to the possibilities of a good relationship. For now, I just want to focus on getting to know her better and not saying or doing anything to turn her off.

I walked outside, sat by the pool and awaited the sunrise. I lay my head back and closed my eyes for what seemed like an hour. I guess I dosed off, because the tap on the top of my head startled me a bit.

"Good morning young man," Cher's voice was music to my ears. "I am sorry I startled you. I didn't realize you were asleep."

"It's okay Cher, I didn't realize I had dozed off myself. I couldn't sleep so I came out to watch the sunrise."

"Looks like I woke you up just in time," Cher's voice echoed in my head. I've waited so long for a chance to really get to know Cher.

I hear rumblings in the kitchen and I'm smelling bacon in the air. Aye the kitchen window is open, and Sade is up making breakfast. I turned around to look at what was happening inside, and Sade winked and waved our way. She leaned out the window to tell us good morning and let us know that breakfast will be ready within the hour. She placed two bowls of fresh fruit just outside the window on the bar counter for us. Cher walked over and got the bowls, and we ate the fruit poolside. Watching the sunrise always rejuvenates me. I could sit on the sand at the beach for hours in silence thinking. Thanks to Stephen, I know that the beach and sitting in the sun is one of Cher's peaceful releases also.

"I was thinking of hopping on Stephen's motorcycle and riding to the shore this morning. Would you like to join me for a few minutes while we wait for Sade to finish breakfast? The shore is only a couple blocks away, but I like to ride the motorcycle and let the sea breeze hit me."

"Say less Jay, I'd love to. This ride will get my blood flowing. The perfect kickstart to my day," Cher explained.

Now if I could figure out how to tell Stephen and Javier that I saw Matthew weeks ago. He was in Vegas. I know the ladies had no clue. If they had Stephen would have flown to town. I saw him and his woman at a private poker game in the Penthouse suite at La Roc, a new hotel on the strip. He introduced her as his friend Grace. I knew immediately that she was more than just a friend. Stephen and Rae had filled me in on the gory details of how he and Cher's relationship ended. Stephen knows talking to me is like talking to a vault. I repeat nothing. It will come up eventually. Right now, I'm just trying to spend time with Cher. Everyone is pissed about Matthew's behavior, but I'm thankful. I never had any issues with him, but we weren't close either. I have wanted to get to know Cher for a couple years, but I chose to respect Stephen and not say anything because he was cool with Matthew. I'm guessing Matthew will come back eventually to talk to Stephen and Javier, but he hasn't yet. Since getting caught, he's been a ghost. I was shocked to see him with Grace in Vegas, mainly because I knew Cher was in Vegas with Vic.

Cher and I arrived in no time. The ride was quiet and peaceful. Now I feel twelve and the butterflies that guys lie about having in their stomach are causing tremors in mine. In my mind Cher is the perfect woman for me. Never married and no children we share that in common. While I would love to have a mini me roaming the earth, I'd be just as happy spending the rest of my life spoiling Cher.

"Hey there, what's on your mind? I can tell you're in deep thought," Cher's voice snapped me out of my daydream.

"Just thinking about how many more excursions I can get you to say yes to." I looked into her eyes, and I swear they were smiling.

"I guess you have to keep asking," Cher said. She winked slyly and leaned over to turn on the portable speaker I brought with us.

I followed her to the shore, blanket in hand. I laid out the blanket while Cher stripped. I know she caught me staring. She stepped out of her ripped daisy dukes and tank top, revealing her ocean blue and sunshine yellow bikini. She slowly walked to the shore letting the tide roll in and cover her feet completely. She turned around, motioning me to join her as she stepped slowly, backwards into the ocean. If I have my way, we will not make it back for breakfast.

Cher turned her back to me and kept walking into the ocean until her body was completely submerged. By the time she came up for air I was standing right next to her with shots of Uncle Nearest Whiskey for us to toast the day with.

"Yes please, this is how you say good morning," Cher sang as she gently took her shot of Uncle Nearest from my grip. "Cheers to new beginnings," Cher's voice was music to my ears.

"Yes, cheers to new beginnings," I couldn't come up with anything better than repeating what she already said, but it felt right.

We made our way back to shore and laid under the sun for hours. It wasn't our intention, but I'm guessing it was exactly what Cher needed. Quietly I needed the escape too. There's no better way to return to center than laying under the sun near the shore with the sound of the waves playing as a sweet lullaby. It's so calming to the spirit.

Awakened by text message notifications we both jumped to our feet. It was 12:30 in the afternoon. Hilarious, we definitely missed breakfast and I'm sure the crew is looking for us. Instead of calling, Cher sent them a group text and included me in it.

Jayden and I hopped on the motorcycle and rode to the shore. It wasn't our intention, but the sun was so inviting, we fell asleep basking in it. We are headed back to the house now. Smooches.

I know we need to help Rae with the last-minute details for Stephen's birthday celebration. I don't want her to be worried or stressed.

"We better start heading back to the house, it's okay that we missed breakfast, but I promised Rae I'd have Stephen out of the house for the day by 2:30 this afternoon so she could finish preparations in peace. The guys and I are taking him to Cooney's for lunch and drinks. After that we will come back, shower and change for the sunset cruise she planned for us all."

"That sounds perfect Jay. I'm so happy for Rae and Stephen, they're great together," Cher spoke with a hint of sadness in her voice. I know her heart is still hurting from Matthew's betrayal. I don't want to push her, but I intend to make sure she knows I am here for her.

"This was a great start to my return home. Thank you, Jay. The hard part is over. I've finally returned home after fleeing from heartache. I won't be here for long, but I conquered the fear of returning."

"You conquered that. The first step is complete Cher, and you can add me to the list of real friends you can count on to have your back. I got you, and don't forget that." I made sure to stare her in the eyes when I said that to assure her, no matter what, I'm here.

Cher has no clue how long I have admired her intelligence and beauty from a respectable distance. She gently placed her hand on my shoulder and squeezed lightly. Then she took off like a lightning bolt and dared me to beat her to the motorcycle. Cher had an interesting way of switching up her demeanor. I guess that's a part of having constantly lived in survival mode. Laughter looks gorgeous on her.

We made it back to the house in no time. We went straight to our rooms to shower and get ready for the rest of the day. I made sure to move too fast for anyone to stop and ask questions about my morning. I assume Cher had the same idea, because she beat me up the stairs.

This shower is taking longer than I expected. All I'm thinking about is Cher. I can't get the image of her coming up out of the ocean and taking the Uncle Nearest shot with me out of my head. She is so sexy! *Shit, Jay, snap out of it!* I swear I want her for so much more than her body.

Chapter 3

Rae

I'll let Cher and Jay have their privacy for now. I'm too busy to dive into their business. But trust me, I'll be getting all up in the mix after my Stephen's birthday celebration weekend is over. I'm paying attention. Jay knows I don't play about my sisters. Once I drop my prince, I will slap these gloves on and deliver beat downs if I must. Damn he's kicking mommy extra today. He must be excited about daddy's party too.

Vic flung my bedroom door open and started looking around. "Who are you in here laughing at? I could hear you in the hallway." The sarcasm ran so easily off Vic's tongue.

"No one Vic, I'm just laughing at the conversations I was having in my head about Miss Cher and Mr. Jay. Definitely no time to get into that today, but honey, they're all mine after the weekend."

"I heard that Rae, I'm with you. I am glad to see her trying to get through this return home as best she can. The wounds are still fresh, so I do admire her for making the sacrifice to return so soon," Vic explained reaching out her hand for mine. I squeezed her hand.

"No ma'am, don't let that tear welling in your eye fall Vic. Today is not the day. We are going to celebrate and be grateful for having each other. We are blessed through all the turmoil sis, we are blessed. I am my sister's keeper!"

"You're right Rae, I love you for always nudging me back to warrior mode."

Vic and I came down the stairs adorned in the new stunning sundresses that she made for us. Each dress was made to perfectly fit our bodies and individual style. I asked her to include my favorite color, aquamarine, in each dress. As always, she understood the assignment and delivered masterpieces. We each had different colors blended with the aquamarine to set us apart.

The guys will meet us at the docks later for our sunset cruise. Before we do that, Sade and I planned a surprise pre-cocktail hour so we can all have a few moments to reconnect and fill up on girl power before we party with the guys. I ordered a driver. The car will be here to pick us up at 4:00 this afternoon to take us to Chanel's Lounge. The Yacht we rented for the weekend is already docked at Chanel's waiting for us when we're done.

"I love you ladies and I know this pregame is for me. Thank you, Rae, and thank you all for loving me, and giving me the breathing room needed to maneuver through my emotions. And yes, thank you too for not pouncing on Jay and me when we rushed in from the beach this morning," Cher shared openly knowing her heart was safe with us.

It's always been a challenge for Cher to trust. I still haven't let her know that I have always known who her grandfather is. I know it's a touchy subject for her and I never want to push her to the brink of shutting down completely.

"We got you Cher, always, no questions asked!" Sade looked at us all to remind all of us she was the big sister, and her words were meant for all who are listening. Sade grabbed my hand and then Cher's in the other. Vic led the way to the pool bar.

"Thanks Sade, I appreciate you for saying that sis, now let's crack this bottle open and take a couple shots before the driver arrives."

"Yes ma'am, Cher, you don't have to tell me twice. Uncle Nearest 1856 here we come. Cheers to good times with great people," Sade said, giving Vic the nod. Vic started pouring the shots.

Our driver arrived after our fourth shot. Of course, my shots were Arnold palmers but who's judging. I'm bringing a prince into the world. I'm high on life right now. I find myself being fascinated with the beauty and growth my sisters exhibit, each in their own way.

I'm so proud of us for how far we've come, and how well we've defeated our individual odds. We are powerful souls each in our own right. I can't wait to watch the *Woman King* movie starring Viola Davis. It is bound to be epic. I planned that as our Sunday afternoon movie surprise.

When we walked into Chanel's our private outside cabana bar was set up and ready for us. I had a personalized signed bottle of Uncle Nearest 1856 waiting for the ladies at the bar with gift bags behind them for presentation. Of course, these bottles were just for show this weekend. There was plenty of our favorite whiskey waiting for us behind the bar. I wouldn't have chosen this establishment if I didn't already know they sold my favorite whiskey.

"This pregame is for all of us Cher. We all deserve to take a breath and feel the peace of being together in the same place at the same time again. I have missed my sisters," Sade said while motioning for us to move closer to the bar.

Our bartender was all smiles when we walked up. "Welcome ladies, my name is Zen. Today's signature drink is the Sunset Passion made with none other than Uncle Nearest whiskey."

I knew my sisters would love it. "Now sit your asses down and start spilling tea! I miss us when we aren't in the same city," Sade quipped.

I placed everyone's gift bag next to them, so they won't be forgotten when we leave for our cruise.

"I'll go first since I am the one about to pop," I laughed.

"You look gorgeous Rae," Vic reassured.

"Honey, I love you, but beauty has nothing to do with me walking around half the time like I'm having an out of body experience. I love my little prince, but mommy wants her body back."

"Welcome to my world Rae. I felt that way while carrying the twins. You're almost at the finish line."

"Thanks Sade, I know sis." I couldn't help laughing inside, because I remember Sade always saying she felt like she was lost in the *Invasion of the Body Snatchers* movie.

"In other news, Stephen and I are doing well. He's been amazing through the pregnancy. He deals with all my mood swings and cravings like a champ. He's the reason I have managed to stay sane."

We know there was a time when it would be believable that I would never be vulnerable enough to settle down with anyone. I still struggle with trust issues. Shit, we all do for differing reasons. But with Stephen I feel the freedom to be exactly who I need to be in every waking moment. His level of confidence in me and the way he wears it himself, makes me want to keep trusting him even more each day.

"Girl cheers to you Rae for breaking down your walls – PERIOD! Know this, I am happy for you and proud of you. I have my own shit emotionally to deal with, but I will. That doesn't take away my joy for you and your love. We all have been through the ringer. I hope you know, even in my silent moments, I'm one hundred percent sure that you have my back. Please know I have yours," Cher pleaded with tears streaming down her gorgeous face.

"Thank you, Cher for letting your heart speak. We know you need to process everything you had to go through with Matthew, and we know it can only happen at your pace. Cher, you're in control of your own healing journey. And yes, we are here every step of the way."

I scanned my sisters' faces and turned my attention towards Victoria. "So, Vic, what's going on with you and mister Victor?"

"Rae, he is a breath of fresh air. No pressure to define our 'situationship' right now. We enjoy each other's company, and he motivates me to keep going on days when my mind wanders to what ifs with Pierre. I relive the night of the explosion often. Sometimes in my dreams, and others in a waking state. At times my mind drifts and sadness creeps in – I see the explosion vividly." Vic lowered her head and took a deep breath.

I know that was a mouthful for her to share with us. I am just grateful she's sharing.

"It's been hard for me to keep my distance little sister, but Vic you know I understand the need to allow change to settle in, hopefully leaving room for you to find peace in your own way," Sade assured.

"Thank you, Sade, you've always known better than anyone how to decipher my moods, emotions and needs," Vic replied.

I put my hand on Sade's right shoulder and squeezed lightly. We had secrets buried deep, there was nothing we wouldn't do to keep each other safe.

"Rae, you guys planned a great evening, we are going to stay positive and focused on future possibilities and blessings," Cher demanded.

"You're right Cher," I answered.

"Sade and I both agreed when planning that we all deserved to have a great time. We are so excited to have you and Vic back on the east coast Cher."

"Well Rae, while I wasn't eager to return just yet, I wouldn't trade our moments together," Cher said holding up her glass for another toast.

Chapter 4

Victoria

Memories of a yesterday that I keep buried lay dormant, for only Sade knows how far I'd really go to save her. We vowed to never tell another soul what happened to her once the damage was done. There was no need to make a public service announcement as some sort of victim. Sade had endured his unwanted advances and acts of molestation, groping and touching her whenever my parents weren't paying attention. After threatening to finally tell our father, Theodore, the monster, scared Sade into thinking that he would kill our mother if anyone found out. The next time our parents left town for a business meeting, Theodore took things to the next level. Angry at my sister for even suggesting she'd tell, he wanted to teach her a lesson, brutally raping her and diminishing her spirit.

I'll never forget the look on my sister's face when I picked her body up off the bathroom floor the night I walked in and found him banging her head against the wall while fucking her from behind like a dog in heat. Hearing her screams and the agony in their cacophony made my soul freeze. Black. Everything was black. And then, silence. I shot the man in the back of the head and watched my sister fall to the floor. I picked her up in one full motion and drove her home.

He never expected me to find them together. I sensed something was terribly wrong with Sade for a while, and I started following her when she'd leave the house. A master locksmith, getting into his home was not a problem for me. He was too busy shouting his filthy demands to hear his door chime as I opened it. The rest has tormented me for years.

I washed Sade for hours, holding her in the shower as her body felt lifeless, shivering. We never told anyone about that night and rarely spoke about it to each other. Sade kept apologizing to me for being too weak to tell dad what was happening when it started. Theodore, was a trusted colleague of my father and he manipulated my sister at seventeen, stealing her trust in men and life. Sade's will to make sure I was okay is the one thing that kept her above water emotionally once this nightmare was over.

We never told daddy. We were mature enough to know that telling anyone in that moment, would only cause further heartache for our loved ones. Mommy and daddy didn't need that. Most of all I know my sister was being quiet to protect me. No matter what, I killed a man in cold blood. And I'd do it again, without question. I felt zero remorse. Only rage for not having known sooner what Sade was going through.

Daddy was there for us on that day without even knowing. If it weren't for him, I wouldn't have known how to kill that monster. Sade and I learned to shoot at an early age. I took more of a liking to it and would go with dad every chance I got to the shooting range. My favorite times were when dad would take me hunting. I was good with a rifle, and I loved the masculinity of Betty, dad's nine-millimeter.

"Hey, Vic, where'd your mind wander too," Cher questioned. Snapping out of my memories, I blinked my eyes multiple times trying to get the eyelash out.

"I'm good Cher, just thinking." The yacht attendant caught my eye and nodded. I think the attendant is signaling to let us know it's safe to get on board when we are ready. Lord knows I'm ready.

"Let's start packing up ladies. Stephen just messaged me to let me know they are parking now. I'll let him know they can meet us on board," Rae suggested.

I am ready to float away for a while. I've been looking forward to enjoying the night sky all day. The temperature is dropping to mid to low seventies, which makes the sea breeze perfect. A welcome distraction. My mind has been drifting back and forth from the night of the explosion when I lost Pierre to Sade's past with Theodore and his devilish son. I need to get back to the peace I relished on the west coast. Although I still suffer from nightmares and occasional daydream sessions from hell, I have found a balance of peace in Vegas and the fresh start it has provided.

Chapter 5

Stephen

The fellas and I are feeling nice and ready to keep drinking. We walked onboard and found the ladies sipping whiskey and jamming to the smooth sounds of nineties R&B, singing at the top of their lungs.

I strolled up behind my gorgeous woman and cupped my hands under her belly. I can't believe I am finally going to be a father. My son and Rae are my greatest gifts this birthday season.

"Hey love, please let the captain know we're ready to set sail," Rae whispered kissing me on the cheek. I sent the captain a text and let him know we were ready. Within fifteen minutes we were cruising the beautiful waters of the Atlantic. Javier came out with plates of food for everyone and placed them on the table for us. We have shrimp scampi, grilled tuna steak, seafood salad and steak. Rae never skimps on food. Since she's entered the last trimester of pregnancy, she has all kinds of cravings and doesn't hesitate to fill them. She's my spitfire and I love her from crown to foot.

"Everyone grab a glass, instead of singing happy birthday to me while hovering over a birthday cake, I would like for you each to offer a toast and share your favorite moment between the two of us," Stephen requested.

"Oh, I love that idea Stephen, I'd love to go first," Cher said raising her glass.

One after the other I got to relive memorable moments with my closest friends. That's what it's all about. Taking the time to live and enjoying the company you keep. We are family.

I cranked up the music after Jayden closed out the speeches. My boy is a good man, never married and no children. He's always working and trying to help others get their footing as entrepreneurs. I'm glad he and Cher hit it off. The two of them becoming friends is a good thing. Cher needs the distraction outside of work, so she doesn't dwell too deep on the heartache Matthew caused. I still hate how he broke her heart. I wish he had left Cher before cheating and humiliating her the way that he did. Cheating with Grace of all people. He can't possibly want a real future with her. Those few minutes of fun and hypotheticals costed him a lifetime with the best woman he could have ever hoped to call his own. But hey, one man's trash is another man's treasure. Cher is a priceless treasure and deserves the best from her partner.

Tonight, kind of makes me miss The Bourbon Princess, Vic's yacht. That night still plays in all our minds - Pierre burning in the fire, with

Theodore. It's hard to gain closure with Pierre's body having never been found. Eventually Vic had the courage to host a small memorial service to honor his life. This was her necessary attempt to move forward. Being in Vegas has truly helped her regroup and remain a vigilant businesswoman.

I'm ready to play whiskey pong, it's one of our party traditions. My Rae gets to designate which one of her teammates drinks for her if necessary since she is carrying my prince. I called out for everyone to follow me below deck to play. The cups were set up in no time. Jayden poured the whiskey in the cups. Before starting we split up into teams and took an initial game starting shot.

An hour later we were laughing so hard, tears began to fall. Victor had been quiet most of the day. He still had work to finish so he was a little distracted from the festivities. It was nice to see him loosening up. Although it's unclear how his relationship with Victoria will end up, I am glad they have each other. Losing Pierre was such a shock for all of us. What he and Victoria had was a once in a lifetime type of romance. Happiness with someone else will always look and feel different. There's no replacing Pierre.

Jayden, Sade and Cher kicked our asses. Victoria, Rae and I were off the entire game. It was hilarious. Vic and I are very tipsy. She turned the music up and sauntered back above deck. Victor followed close behind and they started dancing on the front deck.

Cher and Jayden joined them while I sat gazing at the sunset with Rae. Sitting here makes me think of Pierre. We all haven't been together like this really since he passed. I was a little worried that Vic wouldn't want to go on the sunset cruise and hang out on the yacht with us because of the tragic way we lost Pierre. I figure as long as she keeps busy those memories won't surface right now. If she slows down, we may have a different experience tonight. I'm hoping Victor keeps her relaxed. They seem to be quite in sync with one another.

Javier lowered the music and signaled to Rae that the floor was hers. Oh no, she's got something up her sleeve. She's always trying to surprise me. I should have known she wouldn't expose all of the details of my birthday night. Standing up, Rae took my hand and asked, "Do you remember when you joked about us getting married at sea with our closest friends in an intimate setting?" I looked at her skeptically and replied, "Yes love I do." Just then I noticed Jayden motion for everyone to turn their attention towards Stephen and Rae. Jayden placed himself between us with the biggest smile plastered across his face.

"What is going on Rae?" Rae just winked and looked at me with her mesmerizing eyes. At first, I was genuinely confused, but that quickly turned to anxiousness and excitement. Did Rae just plan a surprise wedding ceremony for me. Why does everyone look as surprised as I am except for Jayden.

Rae turned to face me holding both of my hands in hers and said, "Jayden and I have planned a surprise wedding ceremony for us my love. If you'll have me, we can start the ceremony now."

"Now Rae, how?" Jayden interjected, "My brother your queen asked me to officiate your ceremony since I am a licensed Notary Public in the state of Florida. Legally I am able to officiate the wedding." I turned and hugged Jayden, thanking him. I turned back to face Rae as the tears welled in my eyes and said, "Hell yea, I've been waiting for this moment since our first date. Let's do this baby!"

Vic, Sade and Cher had tears streaming down their cheeks. Javier and Victor brought the ladies some water and tissues. Jayden had prepared a beautiful speech for us, and then moved right into the nuptials. Within fifteen minutes my life changed again. The love of my life is now my wife.

"Rae, this was the best birthday surprise I could have ever hoped for. I'm not sure you'll ever be able to top this one." Rae laughed at me. "You are right husband, it will be hard to top this surprise, but I think you've learned by now not to underestimate me," Rae smirked.

Hmmm husband, I love the sound of that coming from Rae's lips. Wow, we just got married. Let's crank this party back up. Everyone gave a short speech in honor of our union and then we danced and drank the night away.

Waking up the next morning to the soft ripple of the waves was peaceful. I got up slowly trying not to wake Rae. My lower back is wet I must have been sweating in my sleep. I'll shower shortly. I want to go up on deck first to take in the sunrise and think about last night. I heard Rae moan as I walked towards the cabin door to our master suite. It sounded like she was in pain. As I turned around to see what she was doing, she let out a scream that would wake the dead. Screaming and hollering at the top of her lungs she removed the covers, staring helplessly at her stomach. She pushed the covers back and I saw my future pass before my eyes. Rae was sitting in a massive pool of blood. I leapt across the room grabbed my cell and texted the captain to call for emergency help. I explained that it was Rae, and we needed an ambulance waiting when we docked.

I picked Rae up and I hollered out for Jayden, his room was next to ours. I could see the dock from the window, we should be there in a few minutes. Jayden knocked slightly and rushed in the door.

"What the fuck is happening bruh? What's wrong with Rae? Oh shit, the baby," Jayden yelled."

The room started spinning for me while I was holding Rae. Man, you have to get her. Help me man I can't lose my wife." I pleaded, "God Please help us."

Jayden carried Rae upstairs and could see the paramedics waiting. He called out to them, and they quickly got Rae situated and were ready to head to the hospital. As they were putting her into the ambulance Javier, Cher, Vic and Sade ran up to see what was happening. They saw Jayden and I standing covered in blood and the women all ran towards the ambulance. Only I could ride with her. I jumped in and signaled to them to pray and meet me at the hospital. Javier, Victor and Jayden ran to get everything off the boat and packed up the truck. They were in the waiting room with me within forty-five minutes thanks to morning rush hour traffic.

Dear God, please don't take my wife and son from me. The guys huddled around me, and Jayden started praying. His voice was loud and purposeful. No one seemed to care in the waiting room. They bowed their heads and prayed too.

Chapter 6

Jayden

"I'll be back shortly." These were the only words I could muster up the strength to speak after praying with Stephen. As soon as I seem to get to a place of peace, the excruciating pain of losing my daughter weighs on my heart. I've never had the strength to share this with Stephen, or any of my closest friends. If you were in my life at the time, you knew, yet even then I didn't talk about it. The pain was indescribable and there's only so many times one can hear 'it will get better' or 'one day it won't hurt so much'.

Now I must sit through this with Stephen and find the courage to not be in my feelings about losing my precious Jaycee. She was six months old and the center of my universe. I had just finished school and acquired my first plane when she was born. I was determined to provide an amazing life for my legacy. I had mapped out her future. I would have her enrolled in every math and science program I could find and someday, she'd fly next to me in the sky.

I still have moments, many years later, it feels like yesterday.

"Hey man, you good?" Javier asked, tapping me on the shoulder.

"Yes man, I'm good." I tried to respond with a straight face. This isn't about me, and I don't want to talk about it anyway.

"I'm going to go back inside, thanks for coming out to check on my Javier. I appreciate that brother."

We both walked back in together and I regained focus. I buried my emotions and zeroed in on Stephen. Pacing side by side, we looked up at the same time and stopped abruptly; the surgeon was standing before us.

"Stephen, may I speak with you in private." "It's okay Dr. Shae, whatever you have to say you can say it in front of Jayden. We are brothers," Stephen reassured.

"Understood. Sir, Rae has lost a lot of blood, the emergency delivery was too stressful on the baby, we were not able to save him. I am so sorry for your loss."

"But what about Rae," Stephen pleaded, dropping to his knees right where he stood. What about Rae?"

Squatting down to Stephen's level, Dr. Shae continued, "Rae is weak, but she will recover. She will not be able to conceive after this. In an effort to save her life, an emergency hysterectomy had to be performed also. Please know that we did everything we could to save her uterus, but her life depended on it."

Stephen was frozen. He couldn't speak. He nodded and looked up at me.

"I got you man. Thank you, Dr. Shae, it's a lot to process all at once, but we thank you for doing all that you could."

I helped Stephen to his feet, shook Dr. Shae's hand and walked back to where everyone else was waiting. I explained everything so Stephen wouldn't have to.

"How am I supposed to break this to my Rae when the anesthesia wears off. The first thing she will want is her son. What am I supposed to do? How? Why?" Stephen looked into each of our eyes seeking answers, only to find more questions.

Since Rae can't have any visitors for now, Cher let the others know she would call a car service to go back to the house and cook for everyone. It was the one thing she could control, and it would help keep her personal emotions in check. Victoria was committed to staying at the hospital so Sade said she would stay too. Javier and Victor were there with Stephen too, so I decided to take Cher home instead of letting her call a car service. I needed to escape so this was perfect timing.

As soon as Cher and I sat in the car she dove in on me.

"So, why did you really walk off after praying earlier. I can tell something was and still is weighing on your heart," Cher spoke softly.

For the first time in years, I responded honestly. "I'm hurting Cher. This experience opened old wounds that feel brand new. I don't care to discuss this with the others, it's too much for me, but I too lost a child, my daughter Jaycee at six months old. It happened many years ago, yet still feels like yesterday. I had her entire life planned out, and within six months she was taken from me in a fatal car crash. She and her mother died instantly. They were hit by a drunk driver. I never talk about this." I looked over to see Cher's eyes welling with tears.

"Jay, that's heavy. I can't imagine how hard it was for you to be strong for Stephen while trying to keep your pain at bay. I am here for you, whatever you need even if just to listen," Cher said gently placing her hand on top of mine.

"Thank you, Cher." I smiled and flipped my hand over allowing our fingers to interlock. There was something so innocent about our connection.

We pulled up to the house. Cher and I headed straight for the kitchen. Cher passed me an apron and named me her sous chef for the day. Lost in each other's company, jamming to old school R&B and creating a feast fit for royalty was the perfect medicine to clear my mind and refocus my energy. Cooking with Cher is an experience I want to enjoy repeatedly.

"I know we can't leave when we planned but please know that I still want to go on the trip with you. I need a vacation that's not focused on work or personal problems. Jay, I just need to breathe."

"I hear you Cher and I got you, don't ever forget that." Before I could form my next thought, Cher leaned over and kissed my cheek. I gently turned her head and our lips locked. We kissed so passionately; tears began pouring down her cheeks. I tried to pull back, but she pleaded with me not to let her go. I pulled her in tighter and before I knew it, I was carrying her to my room. I laid Cher down on the bed and she sat up immediately.

"Is something wrong Cher?" I was concerned, but instead of answering, she stood up and placed her beautiful hips on either side of my legs and straddled me. In one motion I was at home in the depth of her ocean. In this moment her heart is broken, yet wide open. With words unspoken I know she needs to be in control. Tears streaming down her face, Cher rode me as if it were the last thing she'd ever do in this life. She was in a trance, and I loved every second of her using me to ease the pain boiling inside her heart.

Chapter 7

Cher

The house was quiet, Jay and I passed out after letting our emotions drown in the sweetness of our nectar. It felt good to get lost in him even if for just a few hours. Well, there's something about him. I don't think this will be the last time we get lost in each other. I keep telling myself it's too soon for me to let anyone into even a corner of my heart. I trust no one at this point, and I know that will make for a disastrous relationship. I'm not sure healing is in the cards for me. I just want to feel free and make it through each day with less tragedy than the last. I could tell, however, that Jay had different plans for the progress of our relationship. Determination lives in his eyes.

"Are we good Cher?" Jay sat up next to me on the side of the bed.

"Yes sir, we are more than good." I leaned over, he kissed my forehead and grabbed my hand.

"We should get back downstairs and prepare. They will come home soon. My phone has been buzzing. I am going to check the messages. Turn the shower on so we can take a nice hot shower before everyone returns." Jay smiled and watched me walk to the bathroom. I turned the shower on and let the steam fill the bathroom.

I feel refreshed and ready to do whatever Stephen and Rae need of me. I slipped on my favorite yellow sundress from *House of V* and made sure I touched up my face just a little, so I didn't look so sleep deprived. From Vic's sundresses to Rae's cosmetics, a girl can be made to feel and look gorgeous.

I placed all the food out on the patio table and got the place settings ready. I made a fresh pitcher of white and red sangria and of course there's always whiskey.

"Cher, Javier just messaged to let us know that they are on their way home. Rae is awake but just wants to be alone with Stephen in the hospital for now."

"Okay Jay, I get it. I can understand that. They both have a lot to process."

"This will be one of the most emotional times in their life. Losing a child brings about indescribable pain," Jay exhaled.

I looked at Jay knowing he understood, but couldn't speak on it further for now. He just nodded and picked up two of the shot glasses that I had taken down.

"Hey, no time like the present," I blurted out as I poured two tall shots of whiskey for us.

Just as our shot glasses hit the counter, we heard the garage door opening. That was our que. Everyone was back. Jay and I were both anxious to hear the latest update on Rae's recovery.

Victoria and Victor walked in first with grocery bags. I guess they stopped on the way back to the house.

"I already prepared food, what did you get from the grocery store?" I asked, grabbing a couple of the bags from Victoria's grip.

"We just picked up some steak and fresh vegetables. I was craving red meat and roasted vegetables." Vic thought about her choice of words as soon as they left her mouth.

Sade's ears perked up and she had to ask. "What did I just walk into. Is my little sister having food cravings? Victor is there something I need to know?" Sade asked, squaring off with Victor.

"No and ma'am as Rae would always say. There is nothing you need to know big sister, leave Victor alone." Vic reassured laughing at Victor's facial expression. He was obviously caught off guard. He had zero response.

Javier nodded for Victor and Jay to head outside with him. He knows how to escape the lioness' den.

"Tell us Sade, what did the doctor say before you left." I asked, afraid of what the response would be.

"Physically Rae will be able to come home in a day or two. They just need to monitor her a little longer." Sade took a deep breath and continued.

"Emotionally, however it may take a lifetime to get through the pain and heartache of losing her son. Then the agony of finding out that the surgeon had to perform an emergency hysterectomy to save her life … that's enough to send anyone over the edge. She has to cope with never being able to conceive again." Tears began to fall down Sade's cheeks.

We will all be here for Rae, every step of the way. We always have each other. We will be the strength she needs while healing. I am my sister's keeper, it's what we live by.

"Hey, loves let's go outside with the guys. We all need to eat," I suggested. It was my attempt to cut through the initial silence after hearing the update from Sade.

We walked outside, picked up our glasses and Vic poured a double shot of Uncle Nearest 1820 in each glass. Sade waltzed over to the speaker and turned up the music. There was nothing we could do right now to change the circumstances Rae and

Stephen had been faced with. For now, we can relax and get our minds right. Our brother and sister will need our unconditional love and support now more than ever.

Chapter 8

Victoria

After several shots we let go of our troubles and enjoyed frivolous moments together. The amount of loss we've endured as a whole in recent years can be overwhelming to think about. It's freeing to have moments like this with my sisters and remind myself how far we've come. We are warriors.

Sade and Javier were chilling in the hot tub. Cher and Jay went inside to wrap up the food before going to bed and I was on the patio chase resting on my favorite pillow, Victor.

The sound of what seemed like a cannon being fired startled me out of my sleep. I ran to the window, and I could see a ball of fire at the end of the dock. I turned over to find Pierre not next to me. Pierre, I called throwing my shoes on. I ran outside and bolted towards the yacht. Black smoke filled the air. A ghostly silhouette of Pierre appeared before me. I inched closer and reached out my hand to grab him. I can't reach. I was crying hysterically for Pierre. Pierre please, I pleaded repeatedly. All I wanted was to be in Pierre's arms.

I sat straight up in the bed. Victor was sound asleep next to me. I shook myself into reality. Shit I was dreaming. I keep having this reoccurring dream as if I could've done something to save

Pierre. Why is this happening to me. I'm happy with Victor. Why am I having these dreams. Pierre has been gone for a while now. I miss him, but I have too much to lose to dwell in mourning. My family and House of V keep me happy and feeling grateful despite the challenges to come.

Please God release me from these dreams. Thank goodness I didn't wake Victor. He's so attentive. I can't fathom talking to him about dreams of Pierre. I've been keeping this bottled up inside for a few months now. I have to tell Sade so I can get it off my chest.

I guess Victor carried me to bed last night, because I don't remember leaving the patio chase. I was the first one up, thanks to my reoccurring dream. I poured a cup of coffee and added a splash of bourbon. I went outside and sat by the pool to enjoy the south Florida sunrise. I miss south Florida, but I've grown to love Vegas too. Chateau Vegas is my happy place. Corny I know, but I name my homes now. Chateau Vegas has been my safe haven from the storm that is my life.

I heard the front door creep open. "Who's there, good morning," I called from the kitchen.

"Hey sis it's me," Rae's voice cracked.

I raced from the kitchen to lay eyes on her. "Rae, you're home early," I noted.

"I couldn't sit in that hospital bed any longer. The doctor said if I rest and let others wait on me for a few days then I could come home. I agreed and Stephen assured the doctor that he wouldn't let me lift a finger."

"Okay Rae then follow doctor's orders; relax we got the rest." I fluffed the pillows in Rae's favorite chair and motioned for her to sit.

Stephen walked into the house with Rae's overnight bag and some bags from the store.

"Sit and relax love," Stephen said kissing Rae on her forehead.

"I'll whip you up some breakfast sis. I just made coffee, Stephen if you want to pour a cup for you and Rae." Rae thanked me and sat in silence while I whipped up veggie omelets for everyone.

By the time I finished cooking everyone was up and waiting patiently at the table. I'm guessing everyone is taking their ques from Rae because it's completely silent. I need to break the silence. 'Eggshells' aren't easy to walk on and deep down inside, Rae wouldn't want us to do that. One thing she despises is being treated as if she's fragile or a victim in any way.

"I would like to speak to you all before we eat." Rae spoke softly.

"Whatever you need love," Stephen assured.

"Thank you all for being here for me and Stephen. I'm grateful to have you in my life. It will take a lifetime to heal from this experience, but I want each of you to know that I will be okay. One day at a time, I will be okay."

Rae finished her omelet first and went to lie down. Stephen followed to make sure she settled in and then came back to sit with the rest of us.

Chapter 9

Cher

I don't know what to do. I know I need to be here for Rae and Stephen, but I feel like the walls are closing in and I need to escape. I keep thinking about my grandfather. I'm blessed to have inherited his legacy, and to have the opportunity to change the narrative of our family name. I don't have to live in secret as they did. My businesses thrive because of the seed they planted for me. It was hell growing up without them, but worth the outcome. What I never understood then I am grateful for now.

"Hey beautiful, what are you so deep in thought about?" Jayden questioned, knowing I was a million miles away.

"Ah, I need to get out of here Jay, my head is spinning."

"You've said nothing but a word. Pack your bag. When you're ready we will hop in the jet and go." Jay was such a free spirit. I love how he didn't ask a thousand questions, just jumped into action. I can appreciate that.

I won't leave today, but a long drive would be refreshing and help to clear my thoughts.

"Jay, do you mind if we just take a drive near the ocean for a bit to breathe in the salt air and relax. I don't want to leave Rae just yet, but a peaceful ride would be nice."

"Sure, let me run upstairs and throw on some shorts. I'll be right back down. Then we can leave whenever you're ready Cher."

Jay rubbed the side of my shoulder as he passed by. His touch, although slight, comforts me. I just want to ride and let the wind take my thoughts away.

We drove up the coast to Hollywood beach. I wanted to walk the boardwalk and go down to the ocean. We walked for an hour and stopped at Nick's Bar and Grill for a Bloody Mary and fish dip. I wanted to forget the pain my heart was feeling for Matthew and focus on new beginnings. I'm human though. I still find myself questioning why everything fell apart. I know it's not my fault that he cheated, It was his choice, but still, *why* is a constant question that comes to mind.

"I'm thinking I would like to fly out in a day or so," Jay opened the conversation to see how I felt.

"That works for me. I am ready today, but I don't want to leave Rae on her first day home. I do believe that she and Stephen need a little alone time to mourn the loss of their angel, just not on her first day home. I know Stephen needs us too," I explained.

"Sounds good to me," Jay said.

When we take off, I intend to unplug completely and let silence prevail. I am learning to live in the moment and not let work or thoughts of work consume all of my days and nights. I am mastering the importance of taking *me time*. With all of life's ebbs and flows it's necessary at times to simply *be*.

We stayed out for a few hours. I enjoyed a swim and let the saltwater wash away my burdens. It's something about floating in the sea that feels so freeing. The beach has always been my happy place. Water period really. It's hilarious. I have been swimming since I was nine months old. I fell in the pool at nine months, and I was told that I swam to the edge of the pool on my own and was pulled out. I am truly what you call a water baby.

When I walked back onto the sand Jay was waiting for me on our blanket. I wrapped up in my towel and lay down next to him.

I awakened to find the sun setting. I looked up and Jay was staring back at me.

"I guess I dosed off," I said.

"Yes, love you did, and you looked so peaceful I had to let you enjoy it."

"Thank you, Jay, I appreciate that."

"I keep telling you, I got you Cher," Jay reminded.

I've trusted before and it burned me time after time. I do enjoy Jay's personality and company, I just hope he can truly be patient with our friendship, because it will be difficult for me to completely trust a man again. I don't want to project what others have done to me onto him or the friendship that we are building, but I am one thousand percent guarded. My heart can't take too much more betrayal. Loyalty truly is my greatest asset and weakness.

We packed up and walked back to the car. Jay asked me if I wanted to make another stop before going back to Rae's house. I did. I wanted to get dinner for everyone. We stopped at GG's Waterfront restaurant and ordered dinner for everyone. I didn't want to cook, and I knew everyone would love the food. When we walked in everyone was in the pool except Rae. She was upstairs sleeping. Jay helped me lay out the food on the patio table and made us a drink. He followed me to the hot tub, and we enjoyed the warmth in silence.

Sipping our Uncle Nearest neat we watched the moonrise.

Sade jumped out of the pool and turned the speakers up. She challenged anyone interested in a game of spades. Jay and I stayed in the hot tub and watched Sade and Victoria beat up Javier and Stephen.

I had my eyes closed trying to escape my racing thoughts when a familiar sound cut through the airwaves. "Matthew?" I questioned not realizing the sound left my lips. I opened my eyes to find Jay staring at me. Sade and Victoria stood up. I jumped out of the hot tub. Why was his voice on the radio? It was a sixty-second commercial for his business. Shit if being back home means I have to hear his voice involuntarily I am ready to leave immediately. I walked over to the bar and poured a double and took it to the head. I took a deep breath and waltzed back over towards the hot tub.

Jay stood up and asked, "Are you okay Cher?"

"As okay as I will ever be," I replied sarcastically.

I can't believe this shit. I wonder how long it will take for me to fully be unmoved by the sound or sight of Matthew. This love shit is for the birds. I dunked myself under the water and shot back up.

I guess now is as good of a time as any to let the girls know that I've been receiving weird phone calls late at night. The number is blocked and when I answer I get no response, just dead silence. They don't hang up first though. It seems like the person on the other end just wants to hear me breathe. It's creepy and annoying.

"Hey girls walk with me, I need to talk to you," I motioned for them to follow.

"Your spades game will be here when you return," I promised laughing at the look on Sade's face, she was about to run a Boston on em'.

"What's up Cher?" Victoria asked, knowing I wouldn't have asked them to walk with me if it weren't serious.

"I'm sorry to interrupt the relaxation mood, but hearing Matthew's voice gave me the strength to finally tell you all what's been happening."

"Happening Cher? What are you talking about sis? Dish," Sade prodded.

"Well, every night for the past month I have been receiving phone calls in the middle of the night. There's no caller identified. When I answer, whoever it is sits in silence. It seems like they are just interested in listening to me breathe. Eventually I hang up and it happens a few more times."

"Wait so every night now for over a month this has been happening," Victoria clarified.

"Yes ma'am, every damn night Vic."

"Next time they call you will keep the line open as long as possible and we will have the call traced. I'll be damned if you think I'm not about to get to the bottom of this shit. And one thing's for sure, it better not be that dirty foot bitch Grace fucking with you," Sade continued.

"She's the only person I could really think of that would do that to me. Unless it's Matthew calling to hear my voice. I don't know, I'm just tired of it and I couldn't keep it inside any longer."

"Heard Cher, we got you," Sade said wrapping her arms around me. I held on to her hug for what seemed like an eternity.

"Listen, I know Rae is fragile right now, but I need to get away for a bit. I need to escape my thoughts, work and just be for a few days. Jay and I are going to take a trip. If you need me of course you can reach me. Otherwise, I just need a little time to breathe. I love you ladies. I need the time to remember how to love myself again. I've felt lost in everyone else, which has allowed me not to deal with my own hurt and pain. It's time for me to deal so I can hopefully heal someday."

Victoria and Sade both responded in unison, "I am my sister's keeper, we understand sis. We got you!"

Chapter 10

Grace

I wonder how she will react if I speak the next time I call. I feel like a stupid child, sitting here calling Cher repeatedly in the middle of the night. I can't believe I thought Matthew would want to be with me once there was no need to sneak around. But no, all he does is work and try to come up with ideas on how to get Cher back. I lay in bed at night, now eight months pregnant and he's nowhere to be found. He leaves me at all times of the night, and I swear it's to be with Cher. I never hear anything on the other end when I call her, just a *hello*, then silence.

If he's not with Cher, then who is he spending his nights with? I'm constantly wondering and it's upsetting. Is this my punishment for dating another woman's man? I ruined my friendship with Sade and of course everyone else just to be with his ass. I swear it's the stupidest shit I've ever done. Now here I am with very little and a baby on the way. How am I going to work and provide for my child with no help. I'm terrified that one of these days, Matthew won't return home. Then what? No family, no friends and I severed my professional ties when I betrayed Sade by way of Cher. Those sisters really do stick together.

Going to the grocery store used to be fun for me. Picking out the fresh vegetables and food for dinner, then coming home to cook with Matthew would be the icing on the cake. Lately however, Matthew has been absent and after the other day, seeing Sade in the store broke my spirit. Of course, I couldn't face her. I pray she didn't see me or my huge belly. I feel like I'm going to deliver a ten-pound baby. I'm huge.

I wanted to call Rae and offer my condolences. My former classmate is a nurse at the hospital where Rae was. She was on call the night Rae lost her baby. I'm not supposed to know of course. Being pregnant, I can't imagine what she is going through. I knew my presence would not be welcome, so I said nothing. Now I feel so alone. I have no real support for this bundle of joy that is expected to arrive in just over a month. I haven't heard from or seen Matthew in over a week, which is the longest we've been separated since he's known I am pregnant.

I don't think I can be a mother alone. I have so many dreams left to fulfill. How can I provide a stable environment for my child without Matthew. Yes, plenty of women have soared as single mothers, I'm just not feeling it. As selfish as it may seem, I can't do this alone. I mean really, I don't even know if I could do it with Matthew. Realistically our child is innocent, yet his father doesn't seem to love either of us. After speaking with my therapist, I am seriously considering giving Zaire up for adoption. He's a beautiful baby boy from what I can tell on the sonogram. He should be the center of both his parents' world. He doesn't deserve the negative sentence that comes along with how he came to be in this world. It all boils down to me feeling like I am simply not good enough to be anyone's mother. I'm a homewrecker and these feelings of loneliness that plague me must be karma kicking my ass. Perhaps one day I will be able to forgive myself for the choices I've made, but who knows when that day will come.

With every passing day, I grow more anxious and nervous about motherhood. What was I thinking? I wasn't thinking. I was feeling and being naïve. Now I'm alone sinking in quicksand. I haven't told anyone about my plans to move back to Nassau once I have this baby. I lived there for a few years right after high school. It's time for me to return. I need a clean break from all that reminds me of my mistakes. Zaire belongs with a family that will love him unconditionally and give him the world. All I have to give is heartache and bitterness, caused by my own fucked up choices.

When I'm gone, no one will miss me, so disappearing seems only fitting.

Chapter 11

Rae

I wish everyone would stop tip toeing around me. I think we should all be more concerned about Cher and how she's coping with having her trust broken again by another man. I hope Jayden is gentle with her. I know he wants more than friendship, but with Cher patience is key. I'm glad they are going on a short trip together. It will do Cher good to break away from the sadness and clear her mind. Her heart needs a break.

I've been waking up at night looking at adoption boards. I still want to be a mother. Stephen has always said that he would support my dreams. I never realized how much I wanted to be a mother until I got pregnant and lost the only child I would ever carry. Now I must find a way to bring up the conversation with Stephen about us adopting. I think he'd be open to it, but if he's not, I don't know what I will do. It's so soon after our loss, yet I don't want to wait too long. I want to adopt a son. We have so much love to give. Healing for me looks like pouring my love into a beautiful baby boy that needs it.

"Good morning." Stephen snapped me out of my thoughts.

"Good morning my love. Can we talk?" I asked, willing to wait no longer.

"Yes Rae, what's up babe?" Stephen sat next to me ready to listen.

"I know it's so soon after losing the baby, but I wanted to talk to you about adoption. Stephen, I want to adopt a son. I want us to adopt a son. Healing for me looks like fulfilling my desire to be a mother. I love you so much and I want a family with you." I paused and took a deep breath, staring into Stephen's eyes. Tears welled in his eyes.

"Yes Rae, you had to know I would say yes. I want the same. I want to raise a family with you. You're an amazing woman with so much love to give. Yes! Whenever you are ready, we are ready. I will follow your lead; just know you have my support."

"I love the way you love me, Stephen. I was so ready to be a mother and pour my soul into our little boy. I still want that, and I am grateful to God that there is more than one way to make that happen. If we adopt not only will the child be our blessing, but we too will be a blessing to the child."

"Amen my Rae of sun we will be blessed to be a blessing." Stephen leaned in and wrapped his arms around me, and I whispered, "Please don't let go baby."

Stephen responded, "Never in this lifetime or the next."

We hugged each other tightly. We walked to the kitchen. I fixed a plate of leftovers and went to sit out by the pool. Stephen joined me with a delicious glass of Sade's homemade lemonade.

"Hey everyone," I called. I looked over at Stephen with a smile and he nodded. He knew I wanted to share our conversation about the baby.

"I wanted to thank you all again for being here for us through everything. I want you to share the joy of our latest decision. You all know that I won't be able to conceive and carry a child, and we have come to peace with that. However, my desire to be a mother hasn't changed, nor has becoming a father faded for Stephen. We will be contacting our attorney soon and moving forward with preparing for the adoption process. We will be parents eventually God willing, and you all will be aunties and uncles again."

The look on everyone's faces was priceless. It mirrored relief and excitement. Love filled the air. My village is a blessing.

Chapter 12

Cher

I am happy for Stephen and Rae, but I need to get out of here. I'm excited that Jay and I are leaving today. Matthew has been trying to contact me, and I don't want to deal with him. There's no turning back for me so why bother. I need space to move on. I don't want him no matter how deeply I loved him. There's no getting past the image of him and Grace in my home out of my head. Fuck them!

I placed my bags to the front door so Jay could put them in the car. Our driver is here to take us to the airport so Jay can fly us out of here. We changed our travel plans. Since his schedule changed, he gave me free reign to choose where we escape to. We are headed to Sicily. I have property that was willed to me in Trapani from my grandfather. This trip will give me a chance to see the property and decide what changes I want to make, if any. No one knows me there, so I am looking forward to peace and anonymity. Well, as much anonymity as I can achieve. I have zero intention of advertising who I am, if it's figured out, fine, because I too am not ashamed of my family's past. Of course, we all have skeletons in our closet, but when your own are revealed, it hits different. I've often thought of moving there permanently if the time ever came for me to raise my own family. Hmm, unlikely I know if I can never find a man willing to be true to me.

"You ready to make moves sunshine." The sound of Jay's voice put a smile on my face.

"Yes, I woke up ready," I responded.

"Our driver is close let's say our goodbyes," Jay suggested.

By the time we turned around from the door everyone was walking towards us. Rae reached in and wrapped her arms around me.

"Sis I am well. You don't have to worry about me. I want you to take this time to breathe and let it (whatever it is) all go. Release the negative energy and accept only the energy that ensures your growth and peace of mind," Rae spoke sincerely.

Everyone else approached one by one giving hugs filled with love. I will miss my girls but a get away is just what the doctor ordered for my sanity.

"Sis, get out of here and know that you're in great hands. Jay is a great friend, and he will make sure you have a good time, no strings attached," Victoria said and leaned in to give Jay a hug too.

"Take care of our girl," Vic whispered in his ear.

"I got you little sis, she'll return with renewed energy."

My thoughts took me away for a moment. I felt a slight tingle within. He makes me smile when no one is looking. It's a little scary. I feel like I shouldn't be feeling anything, yet I am loving the energy he brings. It is what it is. I have learned to let the chips fall as they may.

"Alright guys our car is here, we will message you when we settle in Sicily. We're off, love you all," Jay said, ushering me out the door.

Chapter 13

Victoria

Victor and I need to head out also. I hope that's fine with Sade and Rae. I need to get back to Vegas. *House of V* has another location opening in a couple of months. I'm responsible for everything including handling Rae's cosmetics since her product line is sold in all of *House of V* locations. I'm hoping it will bring her new focus and redirect any sad energies back into boss babe mode.

"Sade, Victor and I are leaving first thing in the morning to head back to Vegas. I have so much to do within the next sixty days, and I can't let any balls drop."

"I understand Vic, I got you sis. I will reach out if there is any concern. The new boutique location brings renewed focus to Rae, she will appreciate it in two months when it's time for the grand opening of *House of V at Stapleton*."

"Thank you. I love you, Sade."

"I am my sister's keeper, I got things in Miami, go make moves little sister," Sade said in a demanding yet loving tone. I knew not to question her, just make her proud. Leo and Lea are so blessed to have her as their mother. The twins are the spitting image of her, intellectually and physically.

I'm feeling a little sluggish, and there's no time for that. I picked up a few immunity shots from my favorite juice bar in Wynwood yesterday. Hopefully taking one of those will help kick me back in gear.

"Vic did you let your sister and the girls know that we are heading back to Vegas," Victor asked?

"Yea I just talked with her. She's cool."

"Good, I'm packed we will leave at seven tomorrow morning."

"I never really unpacked Victor so I'm pretty much packed too. Seven works for me."

"I am going out for a run right now to burn off a little stress. I have so much work waiting for me when we return. I'll be back in an hour to shower for dinner."

"I should join you," Victor held my hand waiting for my response.

"No, I need to be alone to think, but I appreciate you having my back. I won't be long. Don't worry."

Reluctantly Victor released the grip he had on my hand. He leaned down and gently kissed my cheek. It's a beautiful day in south Florida. The sunshine will do me good. I'm looking forward to the feast that Sade is whipping up for us tonight.

I'll miss her cooking till we see each other again. I'll surely enjoy every bite tonight.

Sade's stuffed mushrooms and peppers are amazing, and we'll be having steak and Greek salad too. My mouth is watering already. Cooking always makes Sade happy, just like Cher.

One thing for sure is that Sade and Cher deserve all the happiness they can hold on to.

After what Matthew and his bitch Grace put Cher through. I can't imagine what it would feel like to catch my man cheating with another woman in our home. Fuck what it would feel like, I started laughing out loud. I know what the hell I would do. I'd shoot on sight and ask questions later. Crime of passion would be my only defense.

Forty-five minutes of gorgeous sunshine and sweat pouring down my face, I feel rejuvenated. I better head back now so I can jump in the pool before my shower. Rae's house takes up the entire cul-de-sac. As I turned the corner, I noticed something at the front door. It looks like some sort of huge package. I wonder what Stephen ordered for her. He's always surprising her with something. As I got closer, I could tell the top of the package was open. Why would the box be open? The closer I get I hear faint noises. Is it a puppy? Now I'm curious. I picked up speed. The faster I got the louder the noise sounded. I caught my breath and … What the Fuck! I rang the doorbell uncontrollably. Stephen ran to open the door and we both stood there in shock and silence for a moment.

"Vic what is this? Who?" Stephen leaned over as he was questioning me and lifted a beautiful baby boy out of the car seat that was sitting inside the box.

"Shit Stephen he can't be more than a few days old. He's so tiny who would leave a baby here like this," I wondered.

Rae came up behind Stephen to see what all the commotion was about. I know she heard me ringing the doorbell like someone was after me. Before she could utter a word, she noticed the baby in Stephen's arms. She looked into Stephen's eyes and then down at the baby. She reached for the baby. Cradling him in her arms, she walked back into the house. Stephen and I stayed stuck for a moment at the front door. I leaned down to stretch my back and legs and noticed there was a letter in the box. I pulled it out of the box and Stephen motioned for me to open it.

Dear Rae and Stephen,
I know this bundle of joy comes to you as a
complete shock. Who I am is not important. I know

you, and I know you will be phenomenal parents. I love my son; his name is Zaire. I simply am not equipped to be the mother he needs. My life is in shambles, and I am alone. My heart aches, but I know providing the best possible life and home for my son is all that matters. To do that, I have to admit that I am not the person to provide it. Zaire deserves the best this world has to offer. I am sorry for your loss. I can't imagine the pain your soul must feel thinking about the baby you lost. I pray you will see Zaire as a gift from God. There's no question in my heart that the two of you are the perfect couple to pour love and life into Zaire. His health records are taped to the bottom of the car seat. Before shock sets in too deep, I'll tell you here, I put your names on the birth certificate. He's legally yours. It was underhanded, but I went into labor early and I didn't know any other way to ensure he would end up with you, so I lied. I said I was Rae. I wrote her name as the birth mother and Stephen as the father. My name appears on no documents. Who I am is irrelevant anyway. Deciding to have Zaire and trusting the two of you to be his parents is probably the best decision I have made in years. Please don't try to look for me. I am his birth mother, but you two are his parents. I pray he brings you and your family pure joy and happiness. I pray he grows up to be as brilliant and strong as the two of you are. I know he will be surrounded by an extended family full of love. The moment you picked him up into your arms, I turned the camera off that I placed in the box. I just needed to see that he was safe, and now I know he is. May God bless you and the life you will have together. Thank you will never seem like enough, but please know that I am grateful to you both. I have fallen from grace due to my life choices and I hold only myself accountable. Zaire is innocent and I can move on in peace knowing he will never feel the rath of my past mistakes and decisions.

Blessings,

Zaire's Birth Mother

We walked in the house and Stephen handed the letter to Rae. Sade and Javier were sitting with Rae and the baby. Rae passed the baby to Sade as she read the letter. Tears streaming down her face, she reached for Zaire and said, "welcome home." Sade picked up the letter and she, Cher and Javier read it. I ran upstairs to get Victor. I blurted out everything that just happened, and Victor rushed downstairs behind me.

"I love you all, I need a moment alone with Zaire," Rae spoke softly staring into Zaire's eyes.

We all nodded and gave her the space she needed. She walked out onto the back patio, and we watched silently.

Rae

Thank you, Lord, for blessing me with another opportunity to be a mother. I promise not to take this blessing for granted. I will be the best mother I can be. Zaire is perfect and I know you make no mistakes. Thank you for trusting us with your precious gift. Now I know why I haven't been moved to change the baby room. You knew Lord that Stephen and I would have our baby boy, only in your time. Thank you.

Chapter 14

Grace

My flight landed in Nassau fifteen minutes ago. I reserved a rental car so I can get out of here quickly. All I want right now is some comfort food and my bed. It's been one of the most draining days of my life. I never imagined things would turn out the way they have. I haven't heard from Matthew and frankly I don't think he knows I left the country. I packed a small carry-on bag and got out of there as fast as possible. I left a suicide note on the dresser in our bedroom so he wouldn't try to find me if the spirit ever hit him to do so. Frankly I don't think he gives a shit but just in case. In the letter I told him I was renting a boat for the day and once I was far enough out at sea, I'd jump overboard and let the ocean swallow me whole. After a certain number of hours, I knew a crew would be sent out to look for the boat and when located, my body would be nowhere to be found.

He doesn't even know I had the baby. If for any reason he does find me one day, I'll tell him I lost the baby. Technically it's true, or at least that's the story I will share. He wasn't there for me knowing I had no one else so his feelings are not my concern. I must rebuild my life one day at a time, and I can't do that thinking about him and why he treated me so badly in the end. Matthew is dead to me. I have buried my old life. I pray I can eventually enjoy my new one.

"Miss, enjoy your stay in Nassau," the sales rep said handing me the keys to my rental car.

"Thank you," I replied.

Now I must go to my favorite spot and enjoy all the fried conch I can eat on the beach and let the sea breeze take my thoughts away. Giving up Zaire was the best, yet hardest decision I've made in life. He's such a beautiful baby. I hope he never learns who his birth parents are. I wish him a life of confidence and self-awareness. If Rae and Stephen ever tell him that he was given to them, I hope he knows it was done in love. I have fallen from grace, and I feel like I have disgraced my grandmother and her choice to name me Grace. My name in the afterlife that I am about to start living is Dania. The Lord offers grace and mercy. Maybe one day he will forgive my actions, seeing my gift to Rae and Stephen as a selfless act. They deserve to be parents.

Gratitude

Jeff Deshommes, owner of Dez'Noir Photography based in Orlando, Florida has been the photographer for the entire I Am My Sister's Keeper book series. Jeff has been responsible for:
- ➢ Book cover model casting
- ➢ Book cover photography and
- ➢ Book cover design

Thank you for being on this journey.

Let's Stay Connected

The Ocean View Journal:
www.Oceanviewpromotions.net

Bleeding Ink Creatives
www.bleedinginkcreatives.com
inkmebic@gmail.com

I am forever grateful to you for supporting my writing wilds. This has been another labor of love, and I can't wait to share future pen leaks with you. Thank you for reading.

Never forget, you are your greatest asset.
Let no one dim your light. You hold the match that strikes.

With gratitude,

Kilene 'Ki' Williams